CIRCLING THE TRIANGLE

Margrit Cruickshank

CIRCLING the TRIANGLE

POOLBEG

To the Simon Community

First published 1991 by
Poolbeg Press Ltd
Knocksedan House,
Swords, Co Dublin, Ireland

© Margrit Cruickshank, 1991

The moral right of the author has been asserted.

Poolbeg Press receives assistance from
the Arts Council / An Chomhairle Ealaíon, Ireland.

ISBN 1 85371 137 3

A percentage of proceeds from the sale of this book will go to the Dublin Simon
Community.

Cover photography by Gillian Buckley
Set by Richard Parfrey in ITC Stone 10/14pt
Printed by The Guernsey Press Company Ltd,
Vale, Guernsey, Channel Islands

We are the music makers
We are the dreamers of dreams.

Arthur William Edgar O'Shaughnessy
1844-1881

1

I used to believe, each September when we went back to school, that this year was going to be different; this year I was going to get off with a girl, be spotted for my musical talent, stay out of trouble, find happiness at last. In any order. So far, I was still waiting—but you never knew.

So when Rob suggested that I went with him to Helen Donnelly's party, I thought: some day I had to find the girl I'd been waiting for; why not tonight?

The party was on a freezing wet Saturday at the end of November. It was supposed to start at nine o'clock (Helen was that uncool) so Rob and I sloped up to her house at about eleven. She lived in one of these showy designer jobs in Foxrock—you know the type: not quite as big as Dublin Castle, but getting there. The front door was open so we just walked in. I thought of taking off my parka but there didn't seem to be anywhere to put it—and dropping it on the floor for someone to spew up all over didn't seem like a good idea. So I shouldered my way past the snogging couples in the hall and followed Rob into the main room.

It was worse than I'd expected. The stereo in the corner looked as if it had been leased from Windmill Lane and it was belting out (you won't believe this) *Madonna*. The chintzy armchairs and the sofa had been pushed back against the walls to expose an area the size of a tennis court covered in fawn-coloured Axminster. (Or something. I'm no good at these things: our carpets come from Kevin's Karpets down by the station and the nearest they get to quality is their names—*Himalayan Weave, Botticelli Mix* or the one we have in the hall, *Dawn Rise.* Some days I wish it didn't.) The lamps had been draped with red scarves and arranged on the floor behind the armchairs to create what Helen obviously thought was a nice romantic glow—maybe the couples curled up all over the furniture appreciated it, but most of them looked too absorbed in what they were doing to notice.

There was a crowd I knew vaguely, sitting on the floor by the china cabinet, no doubt discussing Life, God and the Meaning of It All. As if you didn't get enough at Life Skills at school. I backed out of the room and tried the one next door. It was a study with a desk at one end, big enough to land Concorde on—and a piano at the other. I went over and ran my fingers up and down the keys. Then I sat down, opened one of the cans of lager I'd brought with me, took a couple of gulps and started to play.

I had just found a melody I thought could be worked up into something interesting when the door burst open and this couple came in practising mouth-to-mouth resuscitation. They didn't even see me. I tried to ignore them but, by the time he'd got her on the desk and was climbing up to join her, my concentration had gone. So I went back into the lounge.

It seemed more crowded than ever. I stepped over various bodies and sat down beside the fire where there was still a bit of wall left to lean up against. Taking another can of lager out of my coat pocket, I started on what seemed the only sensible thing to do: get drunk.

Rob, of course, had disappeared.

The corner I was in was dark, apart from the firelight reflected in the polished brass coal scuttle. The rest of the room became more and more distant. People moved like puppets in it, talking, drinking, snogging, but they had nothing to do with me. I felt apart, as if I was watching a play. I took off my parka, opened a new can of beer, leant back against the wall and found that I was happy: an observer of life's rich pageant. Or whatever.

And then this bird came across. I looked up. She was small and wore tight jeans and a sweater that, even at the distance I was from things, aroused a response. Her hair was black and straight and swung forward past her cheekbones. She looked older than the rest of the crowd.

"Hi. I'm Mandy. Aren't you Catherine Russell's little brother?" From somewhere above the bumps in her sweater, she grinned down at me.

She had a tumbler of fruit punch with lots of healthy kiwi fruit and orange floating on the top of it, which was giving off enough gin fumes to blow up the Customs House. Not for the first time that evening I asked myself where Mr and Mrs Donnelly were and if they knew what was going on in their six-figure, upmarket house.

I tried to concentrate. Mandy? The name was familiar. And I knew I'd seen her before somewhere...Then it came to me: Mandy Donnelly. She'd been in Catherine's class at school—she had to be Helen's older sister. Which didn't give her the right to patronise me. "Get lost," I suggested.

"Charming. Tell Catherine she has my sympathy."

"Tell her yourself. What are you doing here anyway? I thought this was Helen's party."

"I'm supposed to be keeping an eye on things." She grinned. "Seeing that all you juvenile delinquents behave yourselves and don't get up to anything your mammies wouldn't like."

I looked round the room. "You're doing a great job."

"You're a sarcastic bastard, aren't you? Here's me thinking you looked lonely and coming all the way over to cheer you up—I should have known better."

"Thanks, Sister Teresa."

"God," she groaned. "No wonder nobody's talking to you. Excuse me for breathing."

That was easy, looking at her sweater. When that view removed itself, I enjoyed watching her hips as she swayed towards the door. I didn't remember any of my sister's friends being as sexy as that. I thought for a moment it might be worth following her, but then I couldn't be bothered. It was too much of an effort.

The fire was dying down and the people still on their feet were as rare as hyenas in Minsk when I decided to see if there was anything left to eat. I could still walk, I was pleased to note, and stumbled my way across the intertwined corpses, ignoring the curses. I assumed the kitchen door was the one with the light shining under it. I pushed it open. Brightness whammed into my weakened system like an Exocet missile, the fluorescent strip in the ceiling rotated madly and I reached out blindly for support.

My fingers found something soft and yielding which collapsed underneath me onto the floor. Then it kicked me, hard. By the time I had rolled off it, got my hands up to protect myself and recovered from the pain, I could see again.

Mandy was smoothing down her jumper and glaring at me. "I might have guessed. Rip Van Winkle come back to life as a mad rapist. How the hell did Catherine end up with a brother like you?"

I was still caught off-balance; otherwise I wouldn't have tried to defend myself. *Never apologise, never explain*: whoever said that knew what he was talking about. "I wasn't trying to rape you..." I stuttered feebly.

"Oh? So I'm not worth it? Thanks a bunch."

I squinted up at her but couldn't see if she was slagging or not. "I didn't say that...Of course you are. I mean... you're very sexy..." I stumbled on, knowing that I was sounding more and more pathetic. With a blinding flash of intelligence, I saw that the reason I felt such a prat was that she was standing and I was still lying on the floor. If I could only stand up, I'd be able to show her what a superior, articulate, fine person I really was.

I staggered upright, clawing my way up the leg of the kitchen table. When I had reached a roughly perpendicular position, I put my hand nonchalantly on the table to steady myself. It landed on something cold wet and sticky which slid out from underneath me so that I ended up with my elbow on the table, an excruciating pain in my shoulder and my face practically in a puddle of cream trifle. The thought flashed through my mind that the last time I saw cream trifle was at a kiddies' party when I was seven—and that had been a disaster too. Then I heard Mandy sigh, felt her grab my other arm and leant gratefully against her as she pulled me upright again. "You're pissed out of your tiny mind," she said.

I stopped half-way up with my head against the bumps in her black sweater. It felt good.

"Get off," she said, pushing me away. Regretfully, I did as I was told. Anything Mandy told me was okay all of a sudden.

The kitchen steadied down and resolved itself into a bright rectangle of shining white surfaces which hurt my eyes. The table was smeared with the remains of supper and looked like a surrealist painting. I didn't feel hungry any more.

By an incredible stroke of good fortune (*not* usually my lot) there was no one else there so, for once, no one had seen me making a fool of myself. Except Mandy, of course. She had gone round to the far side of the table and was leaning up against the sink, sucking a peach, and looking at me. Seductively.

I ran my fingers through my hair and walked slowly and very carefully round the table to wash my hands at the sink. Mandy passed me a dishtowel to dry myself: her perfume infiltrated my nervous system and short-circuited it. Grabbing her by the shoulders, I tried to find her mouth.

Amazingly, she twisted away and slapped my face. For the second time in five minutes, I hurt.

You know the sort of poor bastards life has it in for— the ones who, if they pour water into a sink, always find a spoon's been left just under the tap or who, if there's one bit of dog-shit in a radius of twelve miles, will step in it and, not only that, won't notice until they're sitting in the classroom with the central heating on? Well, I'm one of those to the power of four million.

Just as I was standing there like a stranded mackerel, trying to close my mouth and rub my cheek and look nonchalant, all at the same time, this fella Mandy's age came into the kitchen.

"You coming back upstairs, Mand?"

And then he saw me. I felt the marks of her fingers stand out on my cheek like a neon light. Five neon lights probably. He glared at me. "What the hell's been going on here?"

I tried to pretend nothing had happened and grabbed a biscuit with white and pink sauce on it as if I was really there to eat. Which I was, wasn't I?

Mandy turned to him, "Get this little creep out of here. He can't keep his hands to himself."

I couldn't believe my ears. The bitch had led me on. She'd come to chat me up in the sitting room. She'd smiled at me. She'd passed me the towel to dry myself. And now *I* was the creep who couldn't keep his hands to himself.

"Sod you. I was just going anyway—you can tell Helen to stuff her lousy party." I spoilt my exit by opening the doors to the utility room and a walk-in larder before I found the back door, which was locked. I couldn't turn the key. So I had to walk past the two of them (he now had his arm round her and both of them were laughing fit to wet themselves, tears pouring down their cheeks) to get back out into the hall.

I remembered my parka and stumbled back across the sitting room to where I'd left it by the fire. A piece of charred wood had fallen out onto the hearth. An idea struck me. A brilliant idea. One of these ideas which only come to you when you're pissed and humiliated and there's nowhere worse to go. I'd show the bitch.

I picked up the charcoal and, using my best mechanical-drawing handwriting, blasted my message to the world across the white and gold paper of the Donnellys' sitting room walls: MANDY IS A SLAG. I had to take down a picture of a thatched cottage and some hills in order to get the last word in, but that was okay: the wall looked better without it.

A few lads were still sober and awake enough to see what I was doing. They cheered me on. One of the girls threw me a lipstick. "Try with that," she suggested.

I did. It was magic. I scrawled more and more obscene messages about Mandy all over the walls till the lipstick wouldn't write any more. People thought I was fantastic. I bowed out of the room to a tremendous round of applause.

All the way down the drive I was pleased with myself. I was the greatest. I'd shown them.

It was only when I reached home and crawled up to my room—after being sick all over the bathroom, something I'd have to pay for in the morning—that I began to have doubts about what I'd done. Nothing, at first, to stop me falling asleep...

Have you ever watched one of these nature films where hundreds of snakes hibernate together in a twisting, squirming knot? If you have, you'll know what my stomach felt like when I woke just after 5 a.m. with my mind showing a video of the previous night. I tried to switch it off before it reached the scene in the Donnellys' kitchen, but it kept on running.

I buried my head under the duvet and wished I was somebody else.

2

At 7.30 I heard my mother get up and go to the bathroom. I crawled out of bed to wedge a chair under my door handle. Just in time. She pounded at the door, shouting at me to get up and clean up the mess. For somebody who intended to go to mass in a couple of hours, she didn't sound as if she was in a proper spiritual state.

I pulled the duvet tighter around me and grunted that I was sick.

"I don't give a damn," she yelled back. "Get out of that bloody bed and clean the bloody bathroom. If you act like an immature infant and come back here and behave like a drunken pig, you can at least clean up your own bloody mess. I did enough of it when you were a baby—I'm not going to start all over again now."

You can tell when she's really out of her skull: the blood is everywhere.

"I'm sick, I told you," I groaned.

"So am I. Sick of you to the teeth. You're coming out of there if I have to come in and drag you out and you're going to clean the bloody bathroom if you have to crawl on your bloody hands and knees to do it."

I pulled the duvet back over my head and hoped the chair would hold. I *was* sick. My head was splitting, my insides were churning, my mouth felt like it was growing hairy mould and all I wanted was for everyone to go away and let me die in peace.

Finally the door stopped rattling. I heard her talking to Dad on the landing, Ma hysterical, Dad soothing her down. He thumped downstairs and came up again. I heard him cleaning the bathroom. The smell of Dettol slunk under my bedroom door and I envisaged him, in his pyjamas, on his hands and knees, cleaning up my sick. It didn't make me feel any better. I turned over to face the wall, wishing they would go away. They did.

I tried to get back to sleep—at least, when you're sleeping, you can't think.

When I was younger, I had this fantasy that I used to tell myself every night—like a bedtime story. I'd be sitting at my desk beside the window and I'd see Clint Eastwood come through the school gates and stroll across the yard. I knew he was coming to get my help: I just had to wait and the Head would come in the door and ask for me. There'd be a short impressive interview at his office, with Dirty Harry standing by, smiling approvingly, and then I'd go off with him to fight corruption and graft. It always started the same way, though I hardly ever stayed awake long enough to finish an adventure. It was better than sleeping pills.

I'd grown out of it years ago—my daydreams now involved more grown-up things, mainly girls. But anything was worth a try now if it would send me to sleep. *Macbeth has murdered sleep.* Mr and Mrs Donnelly have murdered sleep. Mandy, certainly, has murdered sleep. Think of Dirty Harry coming in the gates, me in the classroom looking down, the Head coming in...The only picture that appeared in my mind was the one of me scrawling Mandy's name over Helen's parents' walls. Only, in this version, the others weren't applauding—they were laughing themselves sick.

I jerked over again, put a record on the stereo, turned the volume up and stared at the ceiling. I was just beginning to get carried away when someone started to break my door in again. It was Catherine.

"Shut that noise off! Some of us are trying to sleep."

If you're thinking of having an older sister, don't. Catherine can be okay, but mostly she's almost as big a nag as Ma. I suppose I should have told myself that she'd probably had a late night too, that she'd maybe quarrelled with Mike again, that she might be feeling as grotty as I was myself...But I didn't. I hadn't a lot of sympathy to spare. And I needed consolation as much as she needed sleep—if not more.

I turned down the volume a bit, as a gesture, but not too much: I didn't want to hear the phone—or the doorbell. Would Mr and Mrs Donnelly ring or come round in person? Which would be worse? And what could they do to me? Make me pay for repapering their lounge? I tried to work out how much it would cost. Ma gave me £5 a week pocket-money. So £5 a week for how long? Probably at least a hundred weeks. Two years. I could stand that: you don't need spending money if you're intending to stay in your room for the rest of your life.

An hour or so later a car drew up in front of the house. A white Merc. It had to be the Donnellys'—nobody we knew drove anything as flashy as that.

A man got out of the car. He was round and balding and was wearing tracksuit bottoms that sagged at the knees and a blue-and-white striped sweater that made him look like the Michelin man. Only he didn't have a happy grin on his face.

I told myself it could be a mate of Dad's, somebody selling insurance, *anybody* other than Mr Donnelly, but who was I kidding? I put my head back under the duvet and waited for the worst.

It took a long time in coming. The front door banged again and the Merc purred off. Silence. I went over a few scenarios in my mind: I could run away to England and become a pop star; or join the French Foreign Legion; or maybe the house would suddenly catch fire and I could save the Crumblies and the cat and be a hero. Somehow, I couldn't drum up a lot of faith in any of them.

I heard Dad come upstairs. Unlike the female members of his family, he didn't pound at the door. "Open up, Stephen," he said quietly. "I want to talk to you."

I thought of refusing, but I'd have to face them eventually. Better get it over with.

I moved the chair from the door and hopped back into bed. Dad had his "I'm disappointed in you, son," face on, which screws me up. I didn't ask to be born, that was *their* decision—or lack of one. So why should *I* have to live up to *their* expectations? They've no idea what life's like out there. When they were young, things were different.

If they were ever young at all.

Dad sat down at the end of the bed. "We've all been drunk," he started off. (Oh God, I thought, the "I've been there, I understand it" line.) "And we've all done things we wished we hadn't. But do you realise the damage you caused last night? Not to mention how your mother and I feel, having people come round on a Sunday morning complaining about our son? The whole of the Donnellys' lounge will have to be repapered."

What did he think I am? If he had actually been there,

he'd have known that he didn't need to lay all that on me—I was doing a fine job of laying it on myself. He should also have known that that wasn't the way to get me to admit it. "That's typical," I snarled. "Some fascist bastard comes round and blames me for messing up his capitalistic mansion and you immediately assume I did it. Some parents back up their children. Some parents don't always believe everything they hear about them."

He looked at me. I continued to stare—sullenly, he would have said, no doubt—at the ceiling.

"Well. Was it you?"

"Why ask? You've already tried and convicted me."

"Did you write..." he hesitated, "...obscenities all over the Donnellys' wallpaper?"

"If the great Mr Donnelly says I did, I must have, mustn't I?"

Dad sighed. That's an old one too. Supposed to make you feel sorry for them. I had enough to cope with being sorry for myself.

"Well? Did you or didn't you?"

I thought of taking the fifth amendment, but what was the point? It'd be all over school tomorrow—all over town, all over the world: Stephen Russell fell for Helen's big sister Mandy and wrote her name all over the walls like a total prat. I'd never live it down.

"Uh," I grunted.

"What's that supposed to mean?"

"What's Donnelly going to do about it?"

"You're very lucky. He's not going to do anything. He could sue, you know. He could have you up in court."

"Why doesn't he, then?" That would have been a way out. Being taken to court would be something to boast about. Cancel out the shame. Being sent to prison would be even better—I'd be one of the lads then.

"He doesn't want to 'blight a young life'," Dad quoted bitterly. He'd obviously had to take a lot of flak downstairs and it must have got to him. He's a quiet bloke—Ma says he lets everyone walk all over him. Being lectured at by a rich bastard like Donnelly on how to bring up your kids—I even felt a fleeting sympathy for him. And a twinge of added guilt. Which made me aggressive again.

"Okay. What's going down then?"

"I've agreed to pay for the redecorating, which, I can tell you, I can't afford. It's a bit much, you know—God knows this house needs doing up, and here I am, having to fork out for a decorator just because you can't hold your drink and behave like a yobbo." Dad hates painting. He's always muttering on about one day being able to pay someone else to do it. I was a heel.

"I'll pay you back," I muttered.

"You will," he said. "You are going out after school tomorrow to get yourself a Saturday job. And you're going to work all Christmas, Easter and Summer holidays, until you've paid me back."

"Fine," I said. "Can I go back to sleep now?"

Dad looked as if he was going to say something, changed his mind and went out, shutting the door so quietly I knew he was really mad.

Well? What did he expect me to do? Go down on my hands and knees and crawl to him? Say I was sorry I'd been a bad boy and would never ever do it again?

I buried my face in the duvet so that nobody could hear me sobbing.

3

The next morning I tried the I'm-too-sick-to-go-to-school line, but Ma wouldn't buy it. So I sloped off into town. The story about me and Mandy at Helen's party would be all over school by now—there was no way I was going in to face the slagging.

It was pissing rain—it always is when you bunk off school—so I went to the shopping centre to get warm. Window shopping's no fun, though, when you're broke. I browsed in Ruby's Records until they got suspicious and threw me out. There was a kid there, about ten or twelve I'd have thought, wrapped in one of these see-through pink plastic raincoats that always remind me of a cheap tacky doll my sister Catherine used to have—about six inches long and chubby and faceless with this plastic mac you could take on and off. She (the kid, not the doll—or, for that matter, Catherine) had been hanging about for longer than me. She'd been there when I came in, obviously mitching as well. But *she* wasn't kicked out.

I get mad when people just assume that because you wear a parka and Doc Martens and look a bit scruffy, you're going to knock off their precious goods. They're always going on about looks not mattering and it's the "inner person" that counts—until someone looks like me. The kid had a large canvas bag with her—and everyone knows about these little kids that are left bumming around the street, knocking things off right left and centre, just because they're too young to be put in prison and there's nowhere else for them. I hoped she *was* nicking their sodding records—it would serve them right.

The bookshop was more tolerant. I settled myself as inconspicuously as possible behind a stand of *Asterix* books. I must have been there the best part of an hour before anyone bothered me.

"Are you intending to buy that, or are you just having a free read?"

I jumped about six feet in the air and stuffed *Asterix and Cleopatra* back into the stand. I've always known I blush too easily but, whatever they say, knowledge isn't power.

The fellow in the white shirt and red tie seemed amused. "Why don't you try the library?" he suggested. "It's just as warm and it's got tables and chairs. You'd be much more comfortable." Did nobody ever tell him that sarcasm is the lowest form of wit?

"Er...Thanks," I gurgled and shuffled off. Witty, suave, the master of every situation: that's me.

I'm not too proud, though, to follow up someone else's good idea.

The library was quiet: a little old woman was peering short-sightedly at the titles as she hobbled round the stacks; three men, one old, two young, were reading the papers at a large table and looked like they'd been built in when they designed the place; the woman at the desk was playing with her computer.

I've always read a lot of things just to impress people. I did most of Shakespeare when I was twelve, which impressed people no end. My mother boasted about it all year—still does, in fact: no doubt to help her forget the report cards I bring home. I like Shakespeare. Everybody tries to read *War and Peace*, so I'd decided to leave the Russian novels and concentrate on South American literature instead. They turned out to be great for propping up tables with one short leg or for putting the creases in trousers (assuming anyone *does* put creases in trousers nowadays), but as a read, forget them. I was thinking of trying some of the mega-philosophers next, so when I saw a copy of Bertrand Russell's *History of Western Philosophy*, it seemed a good place to start. It just about needed a crane to lift from the shelf: I hoped the librarian was impressed. I dumped it on the table with a thud, expecting the three blokes to look up, but a neutron bomb would have left them equally unmoved.

Still, now that I had it, I might as well read it, I thought. I skipped through it, from the Greeks to the Romans to Christianity, Schopenhauer and Nietzsche. A couple of quotes caught my eye in the chapter on Schopenhauer. I even copied one down in my homework journal: "Although death must conquer in the end, we pursue our futile purposes." It seemed particularly relevant to my life at that moment. I also copied out one from the chapter on Nietzsche: "Women are not, as yet, capable of friendship; they are still cats, or birds, or cows." It helped me feel better about Mandy. She was definitely a cow.

"Is that a joke book?"

I looked up. The kid in the pink plastic raincoat from the record shop was standing at the other side of the table. A line from Tennyson's "Morte d'Arthur" came into my head. "Clothed in [pink plastic,] mystic, wonderful!" I suggested to her.

She looked at me as if I'd lost my marbles. Then she

turned the book towards her and read the title. "Jesus! You can't think that's funny, can you?"

I admit I was taken aback. I smiled enigmatically. "'To the pure, all things are pure'," I quoted.

The librarian was glaring at us so I flashed her one of the cheeky-yet-charming grins I keep especially to disarm middle-aged women: she didn't respond. I wondered if she was thinking of ringing the guards and having me arrested for child-molesting—she looked as if she was capable of it.

Just as I was enjoying a vision of being hustled out of the library by a couple of culchie guards while everyone else—including the living dead at my table—looked on goggle-eyed, Pink Raincoat spoke again. "I'm thirsty. D'you know anywhere around here you can get some coke?"

I frowned and looked furtively at the librarian. "Shh!" I whispered. "Don't you know you can get life for pushing drugs in a public library?"

"Go fuck yourself."

I looked at her properly. She definitely couldn't have been more than twelve. She stood there in her pink plastic mac, blonde hair falling dead straight half-way down her back, traintracks on her teeth, baby-blue eyes that looked as if they had never taken in anything more noxious than *Bosco* on the telly, using language I'd only started using myself a couple of years ago—and that only in the company of my mates. I began to understand what the Crumblies meant when they went on about the erosion of standards in today's youth.

"There's a café across the street," I told her.

"You coming?"

Was I coming? I looked at her thoughtfully. First of all, I wasn't really into baby-snatching: going to a café with a first year (or was she still at national school? If so, I didn't envy her class teacher) was hardly going to do my street cred any good. Secondly, there was that plastic mac. Thirdly...I couldn't think of a thirdly. And my stomach had been telling me for quite some time that, if I'd been at school, it would have been long past break and heading for the dinner-hour.

"You got enough money, then?" Being seen with her in public was one thing—paying for her was something else.

"Naturally." Have you ever heard a twelve-year-old sneering? It's not an experience I recommend.

She felt inside the neck of her plastic mac and rooted around in the opening of her shirt under the vee of her school jumper. I glanced nervously at the librarian. She had started to stand up. I looked back at the kid. She'd pulled a purse out from somewhere between her non-existent tits and was waving it under my nose. "There's over twenty pounds in there!" she crowed. My face must have registered disbelief because she flipped the purse open and gave me a glimpse of a wad of folded money. Had she been robbing a bank as well as knocking off the record shop? Billy the Kid was nothing on this lady—that was for sure.

The librarian was closing in fast. Plastic Mac grabbed her bag and scarpered. I picked up my own bag with what I hoped was more dignity, smiled at the librarian and followed her out.

We went across the road to the Oriental Café. My mates would all be in school and no teacher in his right mind (or even out of it, which was as well, considering some of our teachers) would be seen dead, as they say, inside it. A pity in a way—there's quite a few I wouldn't mind seeing dead, anywhere. It's not the place to go to either, if you're trying to impress a girl, but, as I said, Pink Mac was about five years too young for my taste. I had decided that she represented a free lunch ticket and I'd be mad not to cash in on it—with all that money, she could obviously afford to spread it around a bit.

I helped myself to two hamburgers and a pile of chips. Okay, I knew it wouldn't do my spots any good, but I needed comfort food after the last couple of days and someone else was paying. I thought of taking milk, to be at least slightly healthy, but in a place like the Oriental Café, you don't know where it's been. I asked for a coffee instead. I let her go ahead of me. As soon as she got to the till, I planned to do my oh-dear-I've-lost-my-wallet act and embarrass her so much she'd pay for us both. I know a gentleman's not supposed to steal sweets from a baby—but I'm not a gentleman and she was definitely no baby.

She helped herself to four gooey cakes and a large coca cola. The cashier rang up the amount. I was trying to use thought transference to make her wait at the counter until I got to the till and started my act, when I saw what she was up to.

I couldn't believe my eyes. Instead of rooting down her neck for her purse, she was feeling in all her pockets with a growing expression of dismay on her face.

"It's gone!" she shrieked. She turned back to me and she actually had tears in her eyes. Hollywood didn't know what it was missing. "Someone's stolen my money, Georgie," she sobbed, loud enough for everyone in the café to hear. "You'll have to pay for my lunch."

Georgie! I felt my face start to burn. Everybody turned and stared. I glared at her. "I'll murder you for this, you little creep!" I hissed.

She smiled back. With her blue eyes and long blonde hair and that see-through plastic mac, she looked as if she should have been stuck at the top of a Christmas tree.

"Come on now, you kids." The cashier wasn't amused. "Get a move on. One of you pay or you can both get out. Hurry it up, now."

I glared at the kid again. I thought of walking out but, now that I had all that food on the tray in front of me, I found my will reluctant to fight the demands of my salivary glands. "I'll pay for my own," I said.

"What about your sister, then?" snapped the cashier.

"She's not my sister. How much do I owe you?"

The kid gave a huge sniff. "You know Mammy doesn't like you lying, Georgie," she said, self-righteously. "I haven't eaten since breakfast and I'm starving."

A motherly-looking woman in the queue behind us gave me a look that would have made Cromwell curl up and go back home. "Here you are, pet. Sure your brother should be ashamed of himself, treating you like that. You just go and sit down and eat your dinner—I'll pay."

"Thanks," she simpered.

The woman turned to me. Her voice took on about forty degrees of frost. "Get a move on then, lad. The rest of us haven't all day."

"I wonder what his Mammy did to deserve him," I heard her say to her neighbour in the queue as I handed over the last of the previous week's pocket-money, picked up my tray and thumped it down on a vacant table as far away from Plastic Mac as it was possible to get.

The hamburgers tasted like chewed cardboard and the chips were half-raw and cold, but people were still looking at me so I had to pretend I was enjoying myself. I concentrated on my plate and ignored the rest of the customers. Just as I was cramming the last congealed chip into my mouth, a rustle of plastic made my blood freeze: Belinda the Kid had joined me at the table.

"Get lost," I snarled.

"Don't be like that. *You* didn't have to pay."

"No. But you made me look a right eejit."

She giggled. "Did poor Georgie not have enough money to pay for his little sister, then?"

"Poor Georgie will cram his fist down your throat, if you're not careful."

"Sorry. But you did look very funny."

"Great. Next time you want some amusement, just look me up."

"Come on, can't you take a joke?"

"Why don't you go back to whatever reform school you escaped from and leave me alone?"

She sat back in her chair with a smug grin on her face. "Don't act so superior, Georgie."

"I am *not* Georgie!"

"What are you then?"

"It's none of your business. Just get out and leave me alone."

"Sorry." The voice was very small all of a sudden. She seemed to shrink inside the plastic mac.

I'm one of these people that stray dogs see coming a mile away. Labradors, Jack Russells, Siberian Wolfhounds, mongrels—they all know a sucker when they see one. "Go home!" I said. "Shoo!" But even as I said it, I knew it was useless. I glared at her. "Why aren't you at school?" I realised I sounded just like Ma.

"Why aren't *you*?"

"I've left. You can't have."

"I don't believe you."

"Too bad."

She was silent for a minute. I finished my coffee (which was cold now too) and got ready to leave.

"Where are we going?"

"You are going back to school. I have other things to do."

"Like what?"

I didn't know, did I? I could broaden my education reading the graffiti in the toilet down by the harbour, lie down on the railway and wait for the next train, throw myself off the end of the pier, go back to the library...The options were endless. One thing was certain, whatever I did that afternoon, I wasn't going to do it in the company of an under-age knacker in a plastic mac.

I was just about to have another try at brushing her off when a shadow fell over the table. The kid went as pink as the coat she was wearing. I looked up.

If I'd thought Mandy was fantastic, goodness knows what class this one was in. Compared to her, Mandy had about as much sex-appeal as a second-hand air-mattress. She was tall and slim with bumps in all the right places, her eyes were sort of greyish-blue, her hair was blonde, her nose okay and her teeth were perfect. The reason I could see them so well, I realised, was that she was smiling very nastily at what, looking from one to the other, was obviously her sister.

"Hi," I said, flashing her a Stephen-Russell-special.

She ignored me. "What the hell do you think you're up to?" she stormed. "I've got better things to do in my lunch-hour than to check all the places you might be when you ought to be at school. Get your things together— I'm taking you back."

"Please, Sue! I can't go back." For the first time since

I'd met her, she sounded like the little kid she was.

Sue. I wondered if that was Susan or Suzanne. I preferred Suzanne.

"If Mum discovers you're mitching, your life won't be worth living. Come on, now. If you make me late too, I'll murder you before she gets her hands on you."

She grabbed the kid by the arm and yanked her out into the street.

I snatched up my bag to run after them: you don't see a vision like that and then let it get away from you. As I kicked my chair back from the table, I fell across Plastic Mac's canvas bag—she must have left it on the floor when she was dragged out. I picked it up and took it with me.

I tailed them all the way to the gates of Grange Park School. Shit. Still, they didn't all have to be toffee-nosed snobs in there—every law must have its exception. As I watched Sue disappear into the school, I felt like Orpheus watching Eurydice going into the underworld: I couldn't bear the thought of losing her. But how could I follow her in there? I hopped from one foot to the other, trying to make up my mind: lust versus terror—mankind's two most basic emotions. Terror won.

I realised I was still clutching Plastic Mac's schoolbag. I looked at it in a daze for a moment and then saw my salvation: with a bit of luck, she'd have written her address in it and I'd have a foolproof excuse for going round to her house (her sister's house!) this evening to give it back.

I retreated down a side road into an empty building site where I'd be safe from anyone I knew. I opened her bag.

My luck was in. Written with indelible ink on the inside was her name, Lynn Carpenter, and her address.

Sue Carpenter: it sounded good. Suzanne Carpenter was even better.

I sat down on a breeze-block, leant up against the wall and repeated her name: Suzanne Carpenter. "Eyes of blue, has my Sue..." I could do better than that.

I spent the afternoon back in the library, working at various lyrics, but none of them was good enough. I couldn't wait to try out a few melodies on the piano— with a subject like Sue to inspire me, I was bound to come up with something great. As I walked home, I could hear my name on the radio, see myself topping the charts, even visualise the song I was going to write about Sue becoming the hit of the year. What the hell? of the decade, of all time.

In fact, as some of you may have realised, I was in love.

4

I had almost forgotten all the hassle over paying Mr capitalist-lackey Donnelly to redecorate his mansion, but I was brought back to reality the minute I arrived home. Nag, nag, nag. First Ma as soon as I stepped in the door: "Have you done anything about a weekend job yet?" And then the action replay from Dad over supper. He's heading for an ulcer the way he concentrates on his worries when he's eating, instead of enjoying his food.

I put them off forcing me straight into the salt mines with the line about too much homework and the Christmas exams coming up, which they were, and which was another source of grief. Sometimes I wonder how any of us survive. I mean they're on to you all the time: cut your hair; tuck your shirt in; clean your room; stop talking; pay attention; stand in line; it's about time you got your act together, young man, you've got your future to think of...

What future? They've been at it since I was five: "And what do you want to do when you grow up?" Make the big time in the music business so's I can have enough money to move out and have a place of my own and get them all off my back, I suppose. But that's not something you tell Miss Carolan in careers. So I'm supposed to be working away for my Leaving and then going on to college. Like one of these geese they stuff food into in France until they burst—only I was expected to stuff myself. And the end result was more likely to be fishpaste than *pâté de foie gras*.

Anyway, having made such a big production about homework, I could hardly announce that I had to go out and chat up a girl that evening. Which meant sneaking out quietly and hoping that nobody would check on my room while I was gone. I've never understood why Catherine and I can't have a key to our bedrooms. They're our rooms, after all. Catherine will be twenty next autumn and she's been earning for almost two years, and yet Ma still treats us both like children. If she ever read any books about psychology, she'd know that every animal needs its own private territory. It's not as if I haven't tried to broaden her mind: I even photocopied an article in the school library once about what happens to rats when they're crammed in a box together. (In case you don't read the right articles, they fight each other to the death.) But she insists that, because she—or rather Dad—earns the money, she owns the rooms and she's not going to be locked out of them. Roll on the revolution.

The other thing was that I had to leave my bike in the hall and go the whole way to Carpenter Castle on foot. And of course it was raining.

Despite the Dalkey address, Sue's house turned out to be more like Carpenter Cottage: one of these little terraced houses down a back street near the station. It gave me confidence.

I knocked at the front door.

Nothing happened.

I waited what I thought was a decent, well-mannered interval and knocked again.

Finally, the door was opened by a tall, grey-haired woman in a black jumper, a long brown and black skirt and bare feet. I tore my eyes away from the bare feet and fixed them on her face, which looked friendly enough.

"I'm sorry," she said. "Whatever it is you're selling, I'd dearly like to buy some and help whoever it is you're helping, but I can't at the moment. Good night."

"Hey! Wait a minute!" I yelped as the door was shut in my face.

I knocked again.

She opened it again. "You *are* selling something, aren't you? Oh no—don't tell me I've done it again. I do apologise—you're a friend of Suzanne's."

It was a statement, not a question. And she didn't seem sorry one little bit.

Which left me with a problem. Either I launched into a long involved explanation of what I was doing on her doorstep with her younger daughter's schoolbag (which she obviously hadn't noticed yet), or I let her go on believing I was a friend of Suzanne's. It *was* Suzanne, I noted.

"Is Suzanne in, Mrs Carpenter?" I asked in my best South County Dublin accent.

"Probably." She turned to shout up the stairs. "Sue! It's another of your bits of fluff."

She smiled at me. I tried to smile back, but didn't feel I was succeeding very well.

"She'll be down in a minute." Mrs Carpenter gave me another slightly absent-minded smile. "I'm sure you'll excuse me. I have work to do." And she disappeared through to the back of the house.

I stood on the doorstep, icy water dripping onto me from a creeper hanging over the door, wondering whether to step in out of the wet or to stay where I was. I decided I'd better stay put—Suzanne might not like my claiming to be a friend of hers (I tried to expunge from my memory the expression "bit of fluff"), and barging into her hall would only make me look more presumptuous.

I heard a door open upstairs, a few bars of classical music—Mozart or something obsessively cheerful like that—and then these legs came down the stairs, long and slim and slinky in very thin black tights. I had to hold on to the edge of the door to steady myself.

Then the rest of her appeared. She stood in the hall and looked at me, puzzled.

"Sorry. Your mother assumed I was one of your friends," I heard myself burbling.

She raised an eyebrow enquiringly. She had fantastic eyebrows.

I dragged my attention back to the matter in hand. "I don't know if you remember me. I was with your little sister in the Oriental Café." Not exactly the sort of dialogue I'd planned, but my tongue seemed to be tying itself in knots.

"No," she said. "I don't remember."

"Ah well. You had other things on your mind." I tried to sound understanding but it came out more as a squeak.

There was a moment's silence as we stood looking at each other. I wouldn't have minded looking at her all night, but she didn't yet seem to find the same compelling attraction in me. I needed to say something witty and memorable—quick.

"Er..." I started.

"Is that Lynn's schoolbag?" she asked.

"Yes," I answered. "I..."

She put out a hand to take it from me. "Thanks for bringing it back."

I held on to it. "That's okay." I thrashed around

desperately for something else to say. "Did your Ma, mother, find out she'd been bunking off school?"

"No, thank goodness."

"She's a strange kid."

She ignored that remark. I wished I'd kept my opinion to myself.

"Can I have her bag, please."

I realised I was still holding it. I let go. "Be my guest."

There was another minute's silence. It was obvious she was trying to think of a way to shut the door and get back to her music and whatever she'd been doing upstairs before I plonked myself on her doorstep. My mind raced: I had to see her again. Unfortunately, instead of coming out as the usual irresistible Stephen Russell patter, the words just whirred around inside my brain, getting nowhere, like one of those clockwork toys already flooding into the shops for Christmas.

"Thanks again for bringing Lynn's bag back." She was edging the door closed.

"Can I see you again?" I pleaded weakly to a panel of solid oak.

Shit!

5

I trudged back home in the pouring rain. The fact that I had to squeeze round Catherine saying goodnight to Mike (in a manner which would keep Mrs O'Flaherty opposite in gossip all week) in order to get in the door didn't cheer me up any: a pair of happy lovers was the last thing I needed.

What did Mike have that I hadn't, I asked myself as I sneaked upstairs, apart from an extra two stone and a bad case of acne? The answer was: a woman.

I lay down on my bed and tried to work out how I could see Suzanne again. Maybe I could pretend to bump into her casually after school...School! Why did I have to remember school now? I'd completely forgotten what a prat I'd been at Helen's party. Would it be safe to go in the next morning, or should I risk mitching another day?

I crept downstairs and rang Rob to see if the Mandy episode had blown over. It obviously hadn't. Rob was still wetting himself over it—and he's a friend; what my enemies were saying didn't bear thinking about. I decided there was no way I was going back to school this century. I got Rob to agree to fix the register for as long as he could get away with it and went back to bed to devote myself to the problem of Suzanne.

It's a great place, bed. It provides a womb-like comfort. Sometimes I wonder if I'm like that fellow Macduff in Shakespeare's *Macbeth*—you know, the one who was "from his mother's womb untimely ripped."

I must have fallen asleep. When I woke up it was morning and I still hadn't thought of anything more impressive than the plan I'd had the night before, i.e. I'd hang about Dalkey station when the schools got out (Suzanne would almost certainly take the DART train home, living where she did) and hope for the best. If I'd been able to spend the day messing on the piano, I might have come up with something better (I always think best when I'm playing) but, unfortunately, Ma's not one of the liberated sisterhood: she stays at home all day to polish the furniture or shampoo the cat or write articles for Greenpeace or whatever. I envied my mates whose mas were out working and who could spend the day in bed or doing whatever they wanted to in warmth and comfort any time they felt like it. I'd have to find a way to fill in the day again.

There was always the library, I reminded myself. If I bunked off for long enough, I might even get myself an education.

I invented an extra after-school pre-exam class so's the Crumblies wouldn't expect me straight home, spent a few scintillating hours with the same three zombies in the library, and got to Dalkey station in plenty of time to watch for Suzanne to come off the DART.

It was incredibly cold. A wind which had started its life somewhere in the Arctic Circle was gusting round the station, whipping the litter into cowering heaps, looking for someone to freeze to death. As train after train came in, all disgorging hordes of schoolkids, none of whom looked anything like Suzanne, I began to wonder if she took the bus. I also began to wonder what the symptoms of hypothermia were and whether there was an antidote. I was just testing my feet to see if there was enough blood left in them to get me out of the station and up to her house (though what I was going to do when I got there, I hadn't thought yet), when I saw her come out of a carriage in the middle of a crowd of juniors. I forgot all about frostbite and sauntered casually after her.

I almost kept on walking when I realised she was hand in hand with the dreaded Plastic Mac.

"Hey, Sue! It's Georgie!"

The train started to move out. For a fleeting moment I contemplated pushing the little perisher under it. I took a deep breath instead.

"Hi, Suzanne!" I said casually, flashing one of my best smiles. "Can I talk to you for a minute?"

"D'you know Georgie, Sue?" Plastic Mac sounded interested.

Suzanne looked at me. "Oh, hello Georgie. You're the person that brought Lynn's schoolbag home last night, aren't you?" Her voice was impersonal: *Good boy, thanks for bringing back the stick: now get lost.* She tugged at her sister's hand. "Come on—we're late already."

I danced anguishedly in front of her. "I'm not Georgie!" I shouted. "I don't know why she keeps on calling me Georgie. I'm Stephen."

"That's even better," Lynn crowed. "Good King Wenceslas looked out on the feast of Stephen..." She wasn't the angel on the Christmas tree, she was the curse of her local church choir. "Stephen fancies you, Sue. Why don't you fancy Stephen?"

Unfortunately, a hole didn't suddenly appear on the platform and swallow me up. I regretted my previous humanitarian instincts: I should definitely have given the brat a good push when I'd had the chance.

Suzanne frowned. "I wish you'd tell your friends to leave me alone."

"Sue wants you to leave her alone," Lynn informed me dutifully. "But you can come along and talk to me, if you like. I don't mind."

The dignified thing to do would have been to walk off. But when has dignity had a chance against love? All the way to her house, I pranced along beside them like an affectionate puppy, trying to convince Suzanne that I hardly knew Lynn; that it was she, Suzanne, that I wanted to get to know better; that I was the type of fascinating, profound, witty, intelligent person that she'd really be into, if she gave me even half a chance.

Lynn was the only one that appeared impressed.

I persevered. Every afternoon that week I walked them home from the DART. I tried every conversational gambit I could think of on Suzanne: I was funny, I was pathetic, I was profound; I talked about Mozart and about jazz; I asked her what books she'd read, what she did in the evenings; I invited her to the cinema, to the theatre, to folk evenings, rock evenings, the National Concert Hall; I suggested taking her to the dog track and the racecourse; I offered to join her watching football, hockey, hurling, darts, tiddlywinks; I thought of everything. Okay, so I had no money—I'd have robbed my blind old granny (if I'd had a blind old granny) if it had meant Suzanne agreeing to come out with me. But no matter what I did, she continued to treat me like a dodgy piece of meat the cat had brought in.

I wasn't particularly miserable. After all, I was seeing Suzanne every day, even if she didn't talk to me. And the Crumblies were happy because I'd invented a Saturday job to give me an excuse to try and see her at weekends. I could hear the rusty machinery creaking away in what passed in their heads for brains: *That shock after the party was just what he needed. We should have come down on him harder earlier. Look at him now, polite, staying in to study after school, and actually looking forward to starting a part-time job! Making him responsible was obviously the right thing to do.*

We didn't reach Saturday, however. Friday at lunchtime, I was sitting on the only decent swing in the corporation dump they call a children's playground off Library Road, eating my sandwiches, and thinking of ways to break down Suzanne's resistance, when who should come in but Rob, looking as if he was half-way round the cross-country course and couldn't take much more.

He shoved a foul-mouthed little brat off the swing next to me and sank into it with a groan. "The things I do for you. I've been chasing round looking for you all dinner-hour. It's not good for my digestion."

"It might help your figure, though."

"There's still hope for mine. One of these days you'll be carted off by a returned aid worker conditioned to respond to skeletons."

I ignored this. "So what's going down?"

"You are, son." Rob grinned sadistically. "The end is nigh. Prepare to meet thy doom."

"What?"

"All is revealed. McCormick checked the register, the

office double-checked and Frankenstein is probably even now on the phone to your aged parents inviting them to a little tête-à-tête in his foul-smelling lair."

"Shit."

"Indeed. Though there are probably more elegant ways of saying it."

Funnily enough, although I had known I couldn't get away with it for ever, being found out came as a shock. Somehow, through one of these incredible survival mechanisms of the human mind so popular in programmes on Channel 4, I had managed to avoid thinking about the future all week. And even now, knowing that all hell was going to break loose as soon as I got home, I was still far more concerned with how I was going to get off with Suzanne that weekend. Okay, so I'd been about as successful as a central-heating salesman in a grass hut up till now, but I hadn't lost hope—somehow I was going to find a way to get through to her. I went back to the library to do some serious thinking.

To my surprise, who should be waiting for me but Plastic-Mac-Lynn, the Scourge of South County Dublin.

"Hi. I was hoping you'd turn up."

I tried not to groan out loud. "What the hell are you doing here? You're not bunking off school again, are you?"

"So what if I am?"

"Suzanne's going to be mad at you."

She looked at me thoughtfully. "You like Sue, don't you?"

I didn't answer.

"I know you do. I've been studying the way boys chase

her for years now and I know all the symptoms. You're just at the early stage—you're not nearly desperate enough yet. And it'll do you no good. I know. You'd be far better off with me. I like having boyfriends."

"I'll bet you do."

"I can kiss, you know. I'm good at kissing."

I believed her. Just in case she felt like giving a demonstration, I grabbed the first book I could see (*Webster's Dictionary*, as it happened) and opened it at random. "Shh," I whispered, smiling ingratiatingly at the librarian. I pored over the book, trying to look as if "pawner" to "pedicurist" was as riveting as a *Playboy* centrefold.

It didn't work. Lynn crackled down beside me and moved the book out of the way. "I've got to talk to you," she hissed. "Come over to the café."

"I'm broke," I hissed back.

"It doesn't matter. I'll pay."

"Huh. Like you did last time, I suppose. I'm not going through that again."

"It's okay. I'll behave. Please!"

She managed to make herself look quite pathetic. And there was always a chance that cultivating Lynn might be a way to get through to her ice-cold sister. "Okay," I said. "But this is the last time."

I picked up my bag and she picked up hers. Instead of the large canvas affair she'd had previously, she now had an even larger rucksack: it must have been games day for her class. Maybe that was why she was mitching? The thought of Lynn, plastic mac and all, playing hockey was too much.

She bought two cokes and six sticky cakes, fished a ten-pound note out of the purse round her neck and paid for them. We sat down.

"Where did you get all that money from?" I heard myself asking. (Do you ever wonder about heredity? I mean, the last thing I want to be in life is anything like either of the Crumblies and here I was, faced with a sub-teen monster, sounding just like Ma once again. It's enough to give you the creeps.)

"Somewhere."

I left it there—which is more than Ma would have done. Maybe there's hope yet.

I took a bite out of one of the sticky cakes. "What was so important that you had to mitch school to see me about it?"

She looked round to make sure that nobody could overhear her, leant over the table to get as close to me as possible and hissed, "I'm running away from home."

I started to grin but, seeing the look on her face, stopped myself. "Oh."

"Aren't you going to ask why?"

"Are you going to tell me?"

"You're supposed to ask. You must be curious."

"I may have other things on my mind." It was an idea, that, running away from home. I'd never have to see the Crumblies or Frankenstein, not to mention Mr and Mrs Donnelly, Helen, Mandy or any of my mates, ever again. But it would mean giving up Suzanne as well. I didn't know if I could face that.

"I'm running away because nobody understands me. They all worry about John because he's sitting his finals this year, and they worry about Suzanne because she gets involved with all these drop-outs, and they worry about Patrick because he's thick and only wants to fiddle with his bike all day, but nobody worries about me. Just because

I'm intelligent, they think I've got no problems at all. And you're as bad—you're not even listening."

"What? Oh, yes. Do you know what Suzanne's doing this weekend?"

"See. I knew you weren't listening. Forget about Sue— she's never going to be interested in you. She's only interested in homeless tramps. I don't know why you don't fancy me. I mean, I'm reasonably good-looking and I'll be even better when I get rid of this brace. And I'm twice as intelligent as her and extrovert and fun-loving and rich—I took all my money out of the Post Office this morning: I've got £80 in my purse. We could get to England on that."

"We? Count me out. I'm not going to get involved in whatever it is you're up to. If I ever go to England, it'll be all by myself, thank you."

"That's stupid. We're both in trouble—we should stay together."

"Who said I was in trouble?"

"You must be. Or you wouldn't be bunking off school. Why don't you tell me about it? I might be able to help— I'm hoping to be a psychiatrist after college and I've been practising for ages."

That was all I needed—a four-foot-high psychiatrist in a pink plastic mac. "Okay then, you asked for it. I killed my father and slept with my mother and now I'm going off to put my eyes out."

She gave me a look that reminded me of her sister. "You think I'm stupid, don't you, Georgie? Of course I know that's *Oedipus*. You're not even funny—d'you know that. You're pathetic. It's no wonder Sue doesn't want to have anything to do with you."

Sue! I stopped wondering how a kid that age could

recognise Greek mythology and thought about Suzanne. Lynn was my only link with her—I had to keep on the right side of Lynn.

"Sorry. I was only slagging," I muttered humbly.

She accepted my apology. "That's okay. I know that some people have to hide their serious emotions behind a façade of humour. Don't worry—you'll grow out of it."

I tried to keep my face straight. "Thanks."

"Girls mature earlier than boys and I know I'm mature enough to put up with you. I think you'd be far better off with me. If you're thinking about running away, then I'd be the best person for you to go with. Nobody would expect to see you with a little sister and, even though I've got the money, I need someone older to go with. I know I look far too young for people not to be suspicious. If we were together, we could pretend to be brother and sister..."

She had to be mad. I remembered her mother's vague look and bare feet and wondered whether the whole family was affected. No, Suzanne certainly wasn't.

And then I knew how to get myself in with Suzanne.

"Okay. You may be right." I smiled, I hoped convincingly. "I've got to go home and pack some clothes. I'll meet you at the mailboat pier at eight o'clock. Oh, and by the way, can you lend me a couple of quid? I'll pay you back tonight?"

She looked suspicious for a moment but I kept my smile nice and innocent. She fished in her purse again and handed over two pounds.

"Thanks. See you at eight then."

I looked back as I left the café. She was still sitting there, a tiny little waif in that dreadful plastic coat, licking her fingers with the concentration of a cat.

All's fair in love and war, I reminded myself. And it would be for her own good.

6

I headed for Suzanne's school and waited for her to come out. She was amongst the last to leave and seemed worried.

"Hi," I said, falling into step beside her. "Are you looking for Lynn?"

For the first time all week, she didn't cold-shoulder me. "How did you know? Do you have any idea where she is?"

"It's a long story and it's freezing cold out here. Come down to Marco's and I'll tell you all about it."

"Tell me now." Her eyes were definitely more grey than blue, I decided. And she looked fantastic when she was mad. "I'm going to kill her when I get my hands on her. She swore she wouldn't mitch again."

"She's okay, but you won't be able to talk to her till this evening. So you might as well come and have a coffee with me while I fill you in."

She gave me a suspicious look. "This isn't just a con, is it?"

I drew an exaggerated X across my chest. "Cross my heart and hope to die—which I will do soon if I don't get something warm inside me. You don't want to have my death from hypothermia on your conscience, do you?"

She smiled briefly. I'd been trying to make her smile all week. It had taken a long time, but the result was certainly worth it. And she agreed, reluctantly, to come for a coffee with me. Things were looking up: half an hour alone with her, without her precocious monster of a sister, would be enough to persuade her that I wasn't like all the other fellows who had fallen for her—I was the true, whiter-than-white, pure, unadulterated, genuine article.

Marco's is near the park. I hoped Lynn would stay at the other end of town, either in the library or the Oriental Café: the last thing I wanted was for her to see me talking to her sister now.

I ushered Suzanne to a table right at the back, just in case, and went to join the queue for coffee, delighted I'd had the foresight to bum some cash off Lynn.

Someone came up and stood behind me. I looked round: it was our form teacher, Charlie McCormick.

"Stephen! How nice to see you again. The broken leg's mended nicely now, has it? Or was it bubonic plague?" He always did have a perverted sense of humour.

"Thanks for asking, sir. I didn't know you cared."

"Ah but we do, Stephen. We do. No doubt you'll find out just how much on Monday morning. I look forward to seeing you then. In the meantime, enjoy your coffee."

I worked hard on the positive thinking as I carried the tray over to Suzanne. She was staring into space, looking worried and very vulnerable. I felt my heart do a complicated somersault inside me and forgot about McCormick.

"Here. Have some of Marco's genuine Eetaliano caffeino. Guaranteed to put hairs on your chest." Stephen Russell does it again. I had a quick debate with myself on whether to try to unsay that remark or just let it lie, like a bit of dog dirt on the pavement.

She hadn't noticed. "You said you knew where Lynn

was today? I've only just discovered she missed school again."

"She's fine. I saw her this afternoon. She's running away from home but she'll be at the pier at eight tonight." To my surprise, no cock crowed thrice.

"Are you sure about that?"

"Absolutely. I got it straight from the horse's—otherwise known as your sister's—mouth."

"The little eejit!" Suzanne looked relieved. "I could murder her. It's typical of her—she thinks of nobody but herself. I mean, here we are, with Dad away in the States, John with his finals coming up any day and Mum tearing her hair out about her Christmas exhibition—and Lynn takes it into her head now to develop a dislike for school. I've had to take her with me every morning and bring her home every evening this week. And now she's mitched a whole day again. How can she be so selfish?"

"I don't know if it's selfishness." I could feel my lips moving and heard this sound coming out of my mouth, but I couldn't believe what I was saying. I mean, here I was, using my first (and possibly only) chance to be alone with Suzanne to talk about her weirdo sister. "She says nobody has any time for her."

"She knows everybody's busy right now. She just insists on being the centre of attention."

"Maybe people are picking on her?" If they weren't, I needed clogs and a pointy hat: anyone who showed off about being more intelligent than everyone else, the way she did, was bound to be knocked around a bit at school.

Suzanne sighed. "I know she's odd—she's always been terribly bright for her age. But she's managed to cope up till now. She has a couple of friends and doesn't seem to need any more. Still...I suppose you could be right. And

I'm as much to blame as anyone else—I've been rushing about for weeks, trying to organise a disco for the Simon Community, and I haven't had time for her either."

I remembered Lynn muttering on about her sister being hung up on drop-outs, and something clicked at the back of my mind about the Simon Community. They looked after down and outs, didn't they? That bottle place at Merrion Gates where Ma'd been leaving in her empty bottles for years (not the sort of person to wait for your local bottle bank to be set up, was Ma)—wasn't that run by the Simon Community? For one treacherous moment I asked myself if Suzanne was really the girl for me: did I really want to become involved with someone who went in for charity work? "Stephen Russell's going out with a Dalkey do-gooder!" I could hear the slagging now.

But none of us is perfect—and the rest of Suzanne was fantastic enough to make up for one little blemish. I decided to carry on. "You're organising a disco? All on your own?"

"Well no, not exactly. But I'm in this group that's setting it up. It's on Saturday—tomorrow. Would you like to come?"

Heaven opened its shining portals: an invitation to the dance. "Tum, de, tum, de, tum-tum, de, tum, de..." The opening bars of Weber's music watlzed through my head. "Sure." Who cares if it's for tramps and drop-outs: Suzanne will be there.

"It's in the Seaview Hotel. I'm afraid it's pretty pricey..." She looked as if she regretted asking me.

"No problem," I said brightly. "How much?"

"Ten pounds."

I was just about to ask how many tramps can afford

ten pounds for a disco ticket when the penny dropped: the disco was for the filthy rich, to help them live with their consciences by feeling that some poor sod was benefiting from their evening out. Well, Stephen Russell didn't mind slumming it with rich bastards for a good cause. And getting off with Suzanne was a very good cause.

"That's okay," I said with, I hoped, more confidence than I felt. "What time?"

"Are you sure you want to go? You don't have to, you know."

"It's for the Simon Community—they do a great job." Did they? Did it matter? "I take it I can get a ticket at the door?"

"Well..." She hesitated. "I actually have some on me. I was trying to sell them to some of the staff at school— we're getting worried about numbers. But please don't feel you have to come, Stephen."

Stephen! She'd actually used my name. Nothing would keep me away.

"I don't have the money on me at the moment. But if you keep me a ticket, I'll pay you for it tomorrow evening." Which would give me a good excuse to get her on my own at the disco. I could see she was torn between delight at having got rid of one more unsellable ticket and guilt at conning someone she thought couldn't afford it into parting with ten pounds: either way I came out well, I thought smugly.

"Are you absolutely sure? I mean, most of my friends said it was too expensive. I'd hate to feel I'd pressurised you into buying a ticket you can't afford."

I put on an air of injured dignity. "I'll have you know we Russells specialise in supporting worthwhile charities—

we're so generous, in fact, that most of the family have to go around with only one arm and one leg." Good, she grinned again. "Anyway, my Ma'll help out. She's a great believer in doing things for other people is my Ma."

Would you believe, I really did think she would come up with at least part of the cash and I even started to ask her when I got home.

"But it's for charity!" I screeched when I could get a word in edgewise.

"Charity begins at home. Charity is not driving your parents grey-haired with sorrow into a mental home. Charity is thinking ahead for once and realising that, if you're in so much bloody trouble for doing something out of school, getting into more bloody trouble in school is not going to make things better. Do you realise the type of phone call I had to take from Mr Franklin today? Do you realise your father will have to ask for Monday off in order to go down to the school and be told what a bloody idiot you are? And you expect me to lend you ten pounds to go to a disco! Sometimes, Stephen, I think you're mad."

"Fine. Good. That's it then. You've made yourself quite clear. Do you mind if I go to my room now?"

Ma sighed. She really sounded pissed off. But I was too, wasn't I?

"Do what you like. I wash my hands of you. God knows what your father will say when he gets home. And in case it needs spelling out," she shouted after me as I dragged myself upstairs, "you are grounded until further notice. Grounded, do you hear."

I didn't bother to reply.

I was less worried about being bawled out by Dad (not that he ever bawls you out—I wish he did, sometimes) than about how I was going to (a) get the money for the disco and (b) get out of the house on Saturday night. Whatever else happened, I was definitely going to the Seaview Hotel. I had promised Suzanne, hadn't I?

I heard Catherine come in and went across to her room. I'd originally intended to touch her just for spending money but, now that Ma refused to pay for the ticket, I'd have to ask her to underwrite the whole evening. How much would I need? Twenty pounds? I decided to try for twenty-five—getting off with Suzanne and then having to be scabby would be the pits.

"What's up with Ma? She's banging pots and pans in the kitchen worse than an African rain-dance. Is the government planning to drive a ten-lane carriageway through our back garden or something?"

"She's found out I've been bunking off school all week."

"Jesus! You really do believe in getting yourself into trouble, baby brother." Catherine looked at me in admiration. "You'd think, one day, you'd quit while you were ahead."

"I'm never ahead. 'Life's a bitch and then you die,'" I quoted. "Anyway, what I wanted to see you about was— can you lend me twenty-five pounds?"

She put her head on one side and looked at me as if I was an interesting laboratory specimen. "You never cease to surprise me. May I ask why?"

"That's my business."

"If I'm going to lend you twenty-five pounds, it's mine."

I thought for a minute. Catherine is usually pretty

discreet. "Okay. It's for a disco tomorrow night."

"For a disco?! He gets pissed out of his tiny mind at a party one Saturday, mitches from school all week and then expects me to lend him twenty-five pounds—twenty-five pounds!—to go and get himself pissed at another party the next Saturday! What's the number to call the little men in the white coats?"

"I have to go," I muttered. Why did everybody make such a big deal out of it? All I wanted was to know whether she'd lend me the money or not—I didn't need another lecture.

She looked at me searchingly. "You're not in trouble are you? Real trouble? If someone's got something on you, Stevo, you'd be far better telling about it than trying to hide it and pay them off. Is something going on?"

"God. You're all so curious. All I want is the money to go to a disco. What's so dreadful about that?"

"Discos don't cost twenty-five pounds."

"This one does. It's for charity."

Catherine let out a whoop of laughter. I wasn't amused. "Since when have you gone in for supporting charities? Unless...Wait a minute. I'll bet there's a woman involved."

"Are you going to lend me the cash or aren't you?"

"So you do fancy someone. And it must be true love if you're willing to fork out that amount of money for one mad night of passion. I hope you're going to bring her back home so's I can meet my future sister-in-law."

"Get lost," I snarled.

When I was back in my room with the door slammed, I realised she still hadn't said whether she'd give me the money or not. There was no way I was going to crawl back out there to her. But, on the other hand...

I swallowed my pride and crawled back. "Are you

going to give me the money, then? I can probably manage on twenty, if you can't make the rest."

She was still grinning. She looked at me sympathetically. "I'm sorry, Steve. I just don't have it on me."

"But you get paid tomorrow."

"I know. But I'm going down to Galway with Mike, so I'll need all the money I have. Sorry."

"Shit."

"Look at it this way, it's probably all for the best. If you get into trouble again this weekend, you might as well leave the country: you will certainly be dead if you don't. And don't say I didn't warn you, brother mine."

I knew that. Going to that disco was like walking straight into a hangman's noose. But the lynching party wasn't till Monday, which was three days away. And anything can happen in three days: I could persuade Suzanne to go out with me once the terminal grounding they would no doubt sock me with was over; I could get run down crossing the road; Sellafield, even, could do a Chernobyl just across the Irish Sea and solve all our problems...

If it did, surely the worst thing would be to die without at least attempting to see Suzanne one last time?

7

After tea, I slipped into the dining room which is where we keep the piano. The Crumblies were watching TV in the front room next door so I made sure I played very softly—the last thing I wanted was for one of them to hear me and start shouting again.

As I said before, I think best at the piano. It's also very soothing. Sometimes, when I'm uptight at school, I'll start playing the top of my desk. I'll ham it up, close my eyes and arch my hands—but I'm deadly serious, really. I can hear the notes going up through my fingers and into my mind and it beats the life cycle of the liverfluke any day.

But even the therapeutic effect of soft piano-playing didn't lead to an instant solution to my problems, the most immediate of which was to find at least twenty pounds, preferably nearer thirty, before the next evening.

Nobody I could think of would lend it to me: Ma and Catherine had already turned me down, Dad wasn't worth trying, none of my mates had that type of money, and though my relations might rise to a couple of quid at Christmas, for the rest of the year they were as miserly as a kiltful of Scotsmen. Which meant I'd either have to nick the money, earn it or sell something. A quick inventory of my worldly goods showed me that I'd nothing left to flog: I'd sold my stamp album when I was ten and the only thing of value I'd possessed since then was my record collection—which I'd converted into a memorable weekend at the Cork jazz festival last year. So that was that. I'd either have to earn it or steal it.

I don't like to think that I'm particularly law-abiding, but somehow stealing didn't seem right. I mean, I know where Ma keeps her handbag (in the bottom of her wardrobe, which is the first place a burglar would look for it—as I would tell her if I wasn't supposed not to know myself), but nicking from Ma was definitely the last resort. So that left earning at least twenty pounds in less than twenty-four hours. There had to be a way.

And then it dawned on me. Music! I'd seen buskers often enough in Dublin—if some of the nerds I'd listened to could make money playing in the streets, so could I. I could certainly play better than most of them. Okay, I couldn't drag the piano into town with me, but I had a mouth organ, didn't I? So all I had to do was find something to collect the money in and get out of the house without the Crumblies ringing alarm bells and locking me up.

I went through and said I was tired and going to bed. Then I thumped upstairs and slammed my door. With a bit of luck, once the frogs in the nature programme they were watching had reached their inevitable mating, the Crumblies would assume I was fast asleep and leave me alone. I put on an extra sweater under my parka, tiptoed downstairs again, removed Dad's tweed cap from the hall stand, eased open the front door, pulled it quietly to behind me, and I was off. Not exactly the start I'd always imagined for my musical career, but you have to begin somewhere.

It was, once again, pissing rain. Naturally. I turned up the hood of my parka and made for the bus stop.

Fortunately, I had enough left from the money I'd scabbed off Lynn to pay the fare into town: after that, it was up to the great Irish public. I knew they wouldn't let me down.

I decided to start in Henry Street—with late-night shopping, it seemed a good place to go. By the time I got there, horizontal sleet was sweeping down from Capel Street, battering the Christmas decorations and making them look about as festive as the miserable passers-by. However, I did my best to think positively: with Christmas just round the corner, maybe people would be generous. I put Dad's cap on the ground, tastefully arranged my last few coppers in it and started to play.

I began with a medley of my own compositions. After all, Hothouse Flowers were discovered when they were busking in Dublin—some famous impresario might just be passing by (maybe that tall fellow in the sheepskin jacket?): if he had any taste at all, he'd realise I was something special and offer to cut a demo disc for me on the spot. The tall fellow disappeared in the direction of O'Connell Street without giving me a glance. Shit.

More people hurried by, avoiding even looking at me. I began to feel I had a notice round my neck saying "Leper" and should have been shouting "Unclean!" and ringing a bell. So much for the legendary Irish taste in music. On the principle of casting slops before swine, I changed to something I hoped they'd like better: "Danny Boy", "Ave Maria", "Shenandoah"...A couple of little knackers made a swipe at the coins in my (Dad's) cap, but they were easily chased off. Someone threw me a 2p piece.

Half an hour later, I had 41p and a Spanish ten-peseta piece.

A fellow about six foot tall in a leather jacket and docs swaggered up the street with a saxophone case. He had spiked red hair and a couple of nose rings. He sneered down at me as if I was something nasty he'd found in the gutter. "Bugger off, scum. This is my pitch."

I continued to play. The notes came out pretty raggedly: "lacking in conviction" was probably the phrase old Williams at school would have used. I doubt if Dave Fanning would have been very complimentary about it either. But I wasn't going to be pushed around—I'd as much right to that particular spot on the pavement as everybody else. It's a free country, isn't it?

He came a step closer. "I said to sod off. Got it, mate? I do this for a living—you go off back to your sodding middle-class home and play with your sodding little computer."

Not for the first time, I wished they'd teach us karate instead of calculus at school. It would be a hell of a lot more useful. I picked up the cap, muttered something about it being a pretty lousy night anyway, and sauntered off.

As I trudged back towards O'Connell Street the bastard started to play. I could hear his saxophone above the guy playing the tin whistle and the women shouting the price of bananas and the fellows flogging sports socks and cheap cigarette lighters. What really got me was that he sounded just great.

I thought about going home, but I didn't even have the money for the bus. And I was still hoping to raise enough money for the disco, wasn't I? So I decided to go up to Grafton Street—it might be better there.

The sleet had gone off by the time I reached O'Connell Bridge. A tinker was crouched on the pavement, a baby wrapped in a shawl on her knees, a toddler hanging onto her coat. She held out a tobacco tin with a couple of coppers in it as I passed. She didn't seem to have done any better than me.

I pulled the hood of my parka tighter round my face. My jeans were wet now too; my feet, despite my docs, like blocks of ice. I stamped them irritably as I trudged on. God, I thought, if this is love, then I'm glad I've never suffered from it before.

Grafton Street was ablaze with garlands of coloured lights and Switzer's window was full of dwarves all jerkily beavering away in Santa's factory. For a moment I was a kid again, brought into town by Ma, excited to be out in the dark, thrilled by the magic of the lights and the tinsel...

I hauled myself back to the present. The street seemed to be crawling with buskers. They were friendlier than the guy in Henry Street, though, and didn't appear to mind someone else muscling in on their scene. As there was nobody outside Bewleys, I stopped there.

I'd just started to play when a security guard came out and suggested I move along: if anyone ever tells you busking is easy, they're talking through a hole in the head.

I trudged down one of the side streets off Grafton Street and tried again. Various people passed by. A woman in a fur coat came over. I tried not to look at her. I was thinking: at least a pound—maybe a fiver. She dropped a 20p piece into the hat. "My son busks, too," she said with a stupid laugh. "I always give to buskers because of him."

"I hope all his patrons are as generous as you, madam,"

I said, leering at her. She missed the sarcasm.

Another ten minutes went by. This old one came up and smiled at me. *Don't tell me your son busks as well.*

"Can you play 'The hills are alive with the sound of music'?" she chirruped.

"Sorry."

"Oh. Still..." She made a great show of taking her purse out of her handbag, opened it, examined the contents carefully and dropped in...5p.

I was going to be a millionaire any minute now.

I played a jazz solo to cheer myself up. A drunk staggered down the alley and rolled into me. He poked his head into my face so that I could hardly breathe for the fumes. "Tha's great!" he enthused. "Really great! Youse is the best player I've heard in...in...Youse ought to be a star!" He held onto my shoulder and felt in his pocket. Taking out an orange note, he stuffed it into the front of my parka. Then he staggered off the way he'd come.

The night seemed suddenly brighter. Okay, so he'd had a bit to drink, but he was the first person I'd met that evening who appreciated my talent. To the tune of five lovely pounds. A couple more like him and I'd be made—after all, I didn't have to buy Suzanne expensive drinks.

I looked at the note lovingly before putting it into my pocket. Then I looked again. Some bastard had taken him for a ride: it was a fake! And not even a good fake at that—just one of these notes that kids use to play shops with made to look like a crisp orange fiver. I keep meaning to ask Ma if she noticed an evil fairy at my christening putting a curse on me.

It was nearly midnight. The pubs were disgorging their last customers—if I was going to make any more cash, it'd have to be fast. I took a deep breath and started playing again.

Have you ever tried to play the harmonica on a freezing cold winter's night when you're soaked through and life has just built you up and then trampled all over you again? I don't recommend it. I tried out some of my own songs again. A few more coppers trickled in, the odd 20p piece, a £1 coin. If this kept up I might be able to pack it in before all my fingers dropped off with frostbite.

Four or five lads came round the corner. I eyed them suspiciously and kept on playing.

They came over.

Their leader, a runt of a guy with bleached blond stubble on the top of a perfectly round head, a squashed nose and a cross in his left ear, leant up against the wall on one side of me. One of his mates (tall, thin, long straggly hair, leather jacket, rolled-up jeans) hemmed me in on the other side. The other three—equally beautiful—stood in front of me, chewing gum.

I stopped playing and looked up and down the street. Up till now there'd been a reasonably steady stream of passers-by. Now there wasn't even a trickle. The good burghers must have got word that there was aggro going down here and decided to go somewhere else.

I tried a smile on Blondie. He smiled back. He was an orthodontist's dream.

I decided to move on. I bent to pick up my cap and the money.

It happened so quickly I was left gasping. The skinny one kicked the cap over to the other three, Blondie grabbed my harmonica and I was left yelling blue murder and holding onto one end of my Hohner like it was the magic turnip.

Beanpole produced a flick knife. I let go.

"Hey, man! I need that money! And that's a good Hohner. Come on, guys. Give us a break!"

Blondie laughed. Beanpole shoved me into the wall. They took off like five bats out of hell.

I ran after them into Grafton Street. I was yelling that they'd robbed me and plenty of people turned to stare, but nobody made a move to help me. So much for public spirit and the milk of human kindness—you could be raped or murdered in this city and everybody would pass by, looking the other way.

The five lads split up. I hesitated, torn between following the money or my harmonica. By the time I decided to go for the Hohner, I'd lost the lot of them.

Why is it there's never a fecking policeman about when you need one?

I went as far as Nassau Street, not really expecting to find them. I was cursing out loud, using every adjective I could think of. But it didn't make me feel any better. I knew I was crying and people were looking at me curiously, but I couldn't help myself.

I spent a few minutes kicking the statue of Molly Malone, which only gave me a sore foot. That was it, then. I was probably going to be expelled from school on Monday, I'd ignored a grounding, I hadn't even the money to get home let alone go to Suzanne's disco, I was soaked to the skin, so cold I didn't believe I could ever be warm again and, worst of all, I'd lost my Hohner. It was the best mouth organ I'd ever had. And a bunch of knackers, who wouldn't have known what to do with a harmonica if it had come up and bit them, had gone off to flog it to some bent shopkeeper somewhere and I'd never see it again. It was too much.

I wandered down to O'Connell Bridge and leant over

the parapet. The Liffey was black and murky. The sleet had come on again and was pitting the surface of the water. I wondered what would happen if I threw myself in—would I drown immediately, or would I freeze to death slowly, swallowing gallons of Dublin's sewage before I went? I was so cold and wet and miserable, I didn't much care.

8

I slumped down onto the pavement, wrapped my arms round my knees and hunched over, trying to keep out the cold. I stared blankly at the pavement. Now and then shoes passed by, black shiny leather shoes, flimsy high-heeled fashion shoes, boots, runners, docs...None of them even slowed down as they passed me. The sleet melted into the puddles on the pavement, fragmenting the street lights' reflections. More shoes passed.

Someone tapped me on the shoulder. "You okay, mate?"

"Sod off."

I felt someone squat down beside me. He smelt like a wet dog.

"I've some hot soup here. It'll, you know, do you good."

I continued to stare at the pavement.

"Pour us a cup of soup, Sue, will you?"

A hand, thick with red hairs, appeared in front of me, waving a white styrofoam cup. The steam was rising from it. It smelt of oxtail soup.

I shut my eyes. I'd stopped believing in Santa Claus when I was five and I didn't intend to start again now.

"Come on, lad. Drink up."

"You shouldn't use styrofoam," I muttered. "It destroys the ozone layer." Ma would have been proud of me.

The fellow took one of my hands and wrapped it

round the cup. "Drink that," he ordered. "We'll worry about the ozone layer later."

The cup wasn't a hallucination. It was hot. I clasped both hands round it and winced as pain shot through my numbed fingers.

"Drink it up, mate. It'll, you know, do you more good inside than out. I'll pour you another when you've had that."

I raised the cup to my lips. Normally, I'd run a mile from oxtail soup—this time I didn't even notice the taste, just the heat working its way down my throat into my chest. I felt like someone on an X-ray screen, as if the progress of the soup down my gullet must be as obvious to anyone outside me as it was to myself.

Your man filled the cup again. "Easy, now. It's hot."

I sipped the second cup more slowly, keeping it as long as possible in my hands to feel the warmth.

"More?"

I took a look at him. He was about five foot square—it wouldn't have surprised me to learn that he earned his living making concrete blocks with his bare hands. He looked the sort of guy you'd hope you never met in a dark alley—even in the daytime. Which all goes to show how deceptive looks can be. I mean here he was actually doling out cups of soup to some unknown nerd huddled on O'Connell Bridge. Maybe this was just a prelude to dragging me off into the white slave trade, but if it was, I might as well enjoy it while it lasted. I held out the cup for another fill of soup.

A pair of legs in black leather boots and tan corduroy trousers appeared behind him. I'm an expert on legs, and these were definitely in the top ten per cent. Life began to stir inside me again. I raised my eyes up past tan knees and thighs to a blue-and-green padded jacket, a tan woollen scarf...

"God! It's Stephen!"

I huddled back down into my parka and prayed that the pavement would open up and let me through. It didn't.

"D'you know him?"

"He's a friend of my sister's."

That was all I needed. I'd been working all week trying to persuade Suzanne that I was interesting, handsome, intelligent and witty, just the sort of person she'd been waiting all her life to go out with. It was typical of the way life mucks me up that, of all the five million or whatever inhabitants of Ireland, she should have been the one to pass by at the exact moment when I was sitting like a prat in the middle of the night on O'Connell Bridge. To be reminded that all I was to her was a friend of her moronic sister was the final straw.

I felt her squat down beside me too. The part of my mind which keeps up a running commentary muttered that all we needed was a cauldron in the middle and we'd pass for the witches in *Macbeth*.

"Are you all right, Stephen? What on earth are you doing here?"

I couldn't look at her. Even in the sleet on a filthy winter evening she smelt fantastic. "I'm doing a survey on footwear." I was surprised I could still speak. "Why else do you think I'd be sitting here?" I attempted to drag myself upright but someone had hollowed out my legs when I wasn't looking and they just crumpled under me.

The hulk put a hand under my arm and helped me up. "You ought to be, you know, getting home, mate. The car's just along the quay there. Do you think you can make it?"

Suzanne took my other arm. A few hours ago, I'd have given anything to be this close to her—why do things never work out the way you want them to? They dragged me along to a clapped-out Escort and I collapsed into the back seat. I wondered if Suzanne would get in beside me—if she did, I would lay my head in her lap and close my eyes and at least die happy—but she got into the passenger seat in the front.

"What about the others, Andy? They'll be expecting us."

Andy took off his coat and tucked it round me. It did smell of dog. I didn't mind—I like dogs. What I did mind was being treated like a baby in front of Suzanne, but there didn't seem to be much I could do about it.

"We'll go round them quickly now. And then take— was it Stephen you said his name was?—home, right?"

I was conscious of the car starting. Street lights flashed overhead, illuminating the inside of the car and shining on Suzanne's hair like a halo every few seconds, and then we stopped again. They both got out.

I dragged myself up and looked through the window. Suzanne and Andy were talking to a large cardboard box in an office doorway. A hand came out of the box and accepted a cup of soup and a couple of packets of sandwiches wrapped in cling film. Suzanne and Andy said a few more words and then came back to the car.

I couldn't believe what I'd seen. I mean this was the centre of Dublin! I wanted to ask if someone was actually living in that box—it didn't seem more than about three feet square, for a start, let alone being weatherproof and providing all mod cons. But speaking demanded an impossible effort—like ploughing through a snowdrift made of cold porridge—and I just didn't have the strength.

I was conscious that we stopped again a couple of times, but things were becoming more and more vague. After that, I remembered nothing until lights flashed on and I could hear, like a nightmare, Ma's voice.

"Stephen! Are you all right? What the hell have you been up to? Are you sure he's all right?"

"He'll be fine, Missus." Andy's voice seemed very far away. "Just make sure he takes a hot shower and get him to bed, right?"

The last thing I remember is more voices and a vague impression of green bathroom tiles...

When I woke up it was daylight. The weather had improved and the houses opposite were bathed in hard, cold sunlight. I could hear people moving about downstairs and looked at my watch. 1.35! I must have slept all morning!

I realised I was starving and swung my legs out of bed.

And then I remembered.

They say a drowning man sees his whole life flashing in front of him as he goes down for the last time. I had the same sensation now—every detail of the previous night came back and socked me, as clear and as cold as the sunlight outside.

I went across to the bathroom to see if there were any sleeping pills in what Ma calls the medicine cabinet. I wasn't all that surprised to see that there weren't. Our medicine cabinet holds nothing more lethal than spare toothpaste and soap, Ma being prejudiced against pill-popping and the rest of us being brainwashed into feeling the same way. There was, however, a bottle of paracetamol tablets, kept there as definitely a last resort. It was worth a try. I swallowed six tablets with a glass of water. They were revolting. I put another four in the palm of my hand, poured another glass of water and tried again. I gagged and spat them out. I put the bottle back.

I went back to my room in disgust: I was too pathetic even to manage to kill myself. Putting on a record, I tried to make my mind go blank. All I could think about was what can six paracetamol tablets, taken all at once, do to you? I went back to the bathroom and looked at the bottle again. "Adults: 1-2 tablets. To be taken 3 or 4 times a day as necessary. DO NOT EXCEED THE STATED DOSE."

Back in bed, I wondered whether six tablets exceeded the stated dose. I waited for whatever was going to happen to me.

Half an hour later, I still felt okay. Deciding I was going to live after all, I got up, dressed and went downstairs.

Dad was at work and Catherine, I remembered, was off to Galway, so Ma was alone in the kitchen. She was beating the living daylights out of a cake mixture. I thought I might as well get it over and done with so I sloped in and opened the fridge.

"Slept well, did you?"

Why is it, every time I feel like being conciliatory, she starts off with some sarcastic remark like that? I decided to ignore her.

"Well? Are you going to tell me why a worker from the Simon Community had to bring you home last night? The Simon Community! As if you were one of these kids who've run away from home and have to sleep rough because their parents don't give a damn. I've never been so embarrassed." I could feel her gimlet eyes boring into my fringe, trying to achieve eye-contact. Long hair has its advantages. "I've always hoped that both of you had enough sense to stay away from drugs," she went on, in that let's-be-tactful-and-assume-the-best tone of voice she keeps for occasions like this. "I take it I've not been living in a fool's paradise?"

What answer did she expect? I removed a piece of cold quiche from the fridge and took a bite out of it.

"Will you bloody well look at me when I'm talking to you! I asked you what you were up to last night—when, in case you forgot, you were grounded!"

I thought of inventing some kind of convincing story but realised that even Scheherazade would have found that difficult. When all else fails, tell the truth. "I was busking."

I could feel her staring at me. "God, Stephen. Sometimes I wonder about you. You really do go out looking for trouble, don't you? I mean, what on earth made you decide to go busking after all the trouble you're in already? Surely you have some instinct for self-preservation, if nothing else? You must have known we'd be mad when we found out."

"If they hadn't nicked my money and my sodding harmonica, you'd never have known," I muttered, trying to justify myself.

She sat down at the table. The look she gave me made me squirm inside. "Tell me I didn't hear that properly. Are you trying to say you were mugged?"

"Uhuh."

"Did they hurt you?" She actually sounded concerned.

"No."

"Well, that's something, anyway." She sighed. I wished she wouldn't. I mean, she's not really bad, as mothers go, and she certainly didn't deserve anything as rotten as me.

One day I'd earn enough money to make it up to her, I promised myself.

I realised she was speaking again. "You know, you'd be much happier if you didn't get into so much trouble," she was saying, rivalling Lynn in psychology. "You really are your own worst enemy."

I don't try to get into trouble, I felt like telling her. It just finds me out. It follows me around like a huge black cloud, just waiting to dump as much shit as it can carry on me. But what was the use? I finished the piece of quiche instead. It tasted like old rubber.

She picked a small card off the table and toyed with it indecisively. "I don't know what to do about this, either," she said. "Or rather, I know what I ought to do..."

"What is it?" I asked, trying to sound interested. It was the least I could do.

"It's an invitation to a charity disco tonight for the Simon Community. Suzanne Carpenter brought it round."

Suzanne was here? I thought, then I realised I'd said it out loud.

"She told me you'd been intending to go and she hoped you hadn't changed your mind. She said you needn't pay her for it, but if we're going to accept it, we obviously can't take it for nothing."

What did she mean "if we're going to accept it"? She couldn't be intending to let me go to the disco, could she? Had worrying about me finally blown her mind? I risked a direct glance at her: she looked anxious but not insane— an impression confirmed by her next remark.

"There is obviously no way you are going to that disco—not after all the trouble you've caused."

That was that then: life was back to normal and miracles didn't exist—or not for me, anyway. But Ma was still rabbiting on. "On the other hand, the Carpenters are a very nice family—Amy Carpenter is in Greenpeace with me, and Suzanne is a very sweet girl. It's a pity you don't have a girlfriend like her, a nice well-mannered young person involved in charity work—it'd do you no harm to spend a bit of time helping others for a change instead of spending all your days thumping that bloody piano."

Ma is a great believer in the civilising power of a good woman. I sometimes wonder if Dad was a loutish yob before he met her. I doubt it, though. In fact, I doubt very much if anything Ma ever said made a blind bit of difference to him. He's stubborn in his own quiet way, is my dad.

What the hell was I thinking about Dad for now? Suzanne had been in my house! She'd come here specially to see me! "What did she say? Why didn't you wake me up?"

Ma grinned infuriatingly. "Aha. So there is something going on between you. I wondered, when she came round this morning, asking after you."

I remembered what a prat I'd looked last night. But maybe she'd seen me differently. Everyone knows that inside every girl there's a Florence Nightingale just dying to get out—and she actually went in for helping the poor and the needy. Maybe I'd appealed to her maternal instinct or something. It wasn't the way I wanted to appeal to her, but it would be a start. It would give her a chance to get to know me better and discover the real Stephen Russell, the man behind the mask.

"It puts me in a bit of a spot, though," Ma went on. "I mean, I'd like to support the Simon Community and if the Carpenters are involved..." She tailed off indecisively. Could she be hearing Mendelssohn's "Wedding March" in her mind? I managed to suppress a grin.

"I wouldn't have been able to go anyway," I said, trying to sound suitably martyred. "The tickets cost ten pounds and then I'd need something extra to look after Suzanne properly..." That sounded good, I felt. "There's no way I can raise that kind of money by this evening, even if you let me go."

"Is that why you sneaked out last night? To try to raise the money?"

"Well, yes. It's a good cause, as you said yourself. I mean, the Simon Community do an awful lot of good work." I didn't bother to point out that one of their good works was to bring her only son home last night—it didn't seem to be a great idea to remind her of the past just when she was starting to think positively about the night to come.

"Well...Maybe. I suppose I could pay for the ticket. After all, they did drive you all the way back here, last night." I might have guessed she wouldn't forget so easily. "And I suppose I could lend you next week's pocket-money in advance..."

Don't remember Mr Donnelly now, I prayed. She didn't.

"All right, then. Seeing as we really do owe them something, I'll let you go this time. But I warn you, Stephen. If you get into any trouble at all, I'll never give you the benefit of the doubt again. I'm trusting you to behave yourself. And to be home early—I want you back here by 11.30, do you hear? One minute later and you will be grounded for life. I mean that."

"Okay, Mum. 11.30. I promise."

I nearly gave her a hug—but that might have destroyed the fragile relationship we've been building up for nearly seventeen years, so I restrained myself and went through to the dining room. I was going to see Suzanne again tonight! And she had actually come round to the house to persuade me to go to her disco. Me, Stephen Russell, whom she had hardly addressed two words to all week!

Despite Ma's suspicions, I've never tried drugs. But playing the piano that afternoon I knew what it felt like to be on an absolute high.

9

I had a shower. Dad's bottle of aftershave was on the bathroom window ledge, so I splashed it round my face and neck and under my arms—you don't have to join the boy scouts to believe in being prepared. By the time I'd dressed, I realised I'd gone a bit over the top but it was too late to do anything about it—I hoped the pong would have worn off by the time I reached Dun Laoghaire.

I stuck my head round the door of the front room. Dad looked up and sniffed exaggeratedly. "Now I know what they mean by chemical warfare. I wouldn't let her get too close, son, if I was you: you could be had up for murder."

"Don't listen to him, Stephen. You look very nice. Have a good time—and remember now, be back at 11.30 at the very latest."

They had obviously decided to pretend to forget about my disgrace and act as if it was a normal Saturday night. I was only too delighted to go along with them. "No problem. You have a good time too." I grinned at Ma and looked pointedly at Dad, sunk in his armchair, his feet in brown leather slippers, an old grey cardigan over his Saturday shirt, just dying to get back to the telly. "I'd watch him, though. Just remember, there's nobody in the house to protect you if he gets randy."

"One of these days, Stephen, you'll go too far. Just you make sure you behave yourself with Suzanne."

I only hoped I'd get the chance.